Shadow of Darcy: A Sensual Pride & Prejudice Paranormal Variation

Abbey North

Published by Abbey North JAFF Books, 2021.

SHADOW OF DARCY: A SENSUAL PRIDE & PREJUDICE PARANORMAL VARIATION

First edition. August 7, 2021.

Copyright © 2021 Abbey North.

ISBN: 979-8215018804

Written by Abbey North.

Blurb

Will Lizzy lose her heart or her life to the enigmatic Mr. Darcy?

Lizzy is the newest instructor at Netherfield Academy, and strange noises have her searching the corridors of the drafty old castle to discover the source. The previous headmaster disappeared under strange circumstances, and when his replacement, Mr. Darcy, catches her in the corridors, he warns her. The first time. The next time, he kisses her, and she sees something different about him. Darcy is as mysterious as the surroundings, and she fears for her life, her sanity, and her heart as she strives to resist the pull he exerts on her.

This is a paranormal take on ODC with a strong dash of gothic as well. While Abbey sometimes writes sweet JAFF, this is strictly SENSUAL.

Chapter One

Lizzy's eyes sprang open as she heard a furtive sound. It was followed by a noise almost like a groan or howl. She shuddered in her bed and contemplated ignoring the commotion. That was the wise thing to do, but if someone were in distress, was it her duty as the music instructor at Netherfield Academy to check on the girls? They were in the other wing, but she still felt compelled to investigate.

She'd only been at the academy for a week, but Lizzy intended to take her position very seriously. She had been lucky to obtain the job as it were, thanks mainly to her sister's connection to the academy, already employed there. Jane, who was also her roommate, currently snored softly in the bed across the room, so Lizzy didn't wake her to find out if she had heard the noise. Clearly, Jane hadn't.

Feeling nervous, but telling herself she was being ridiculously timid, Lizzy slid out of bed and put her feet into slippers before reaching for her night-rail. She wrapped it around her thick flannel gown, still shivering in the chilly air. The old castle housing Netherfield Academy was cold and drafty, and Jane had told her it was like that sometimes even in summer.

Lizzy would have to adapt, since she'd lived the last two years in London studying at a musical conservatory. London was cold in winter, but it was dreadfully hot in summer sometimes, so it would be a refreshing change to spend a cooler summer here in the wilds of Northern England, assuming she got past how disquieting the castle was.

Lizzy paused long enough to light a candelabra to guide her way before leaving her room. She hesitated at the doorway for a long moment, half-convinced she must have imagined things. She was on the verge of returning to her bed when she heard the sound again. It was certainly a low, anguished groan. Someone was in pain, though it didn't appear to come from the wing of the castle housing students.

Before she could be torn apart by indecision, Lizzy acquiesced to her normal curiosity and started walking down the hall, in search of the source of the noise. It wasn't from any of the staff rooms near hers, but as she moved farther down the wing, it grew louder and more consistent. She reached a bend in the corridor, pausing for a moment to determine which direction she should go.

A cold hand grasped her arm, making her scream and jump in shock at the same time. That same hand covered her mouth, and she started to struggle. "Calm down, Miss Bennet. I am simply keeping you from shouting the entire castle awake."

She shivered as she recognized the voice of the headmaster, Fitzwilliam Darcy. She'd met him only once briefly the first day she'd started at the academy, when she arrived that evening. It had been a long journey, so their meeting had been brief, but she immediately recalled how handsome he was. She'd chastised herself for the thought at the time and did so anew as she turned to face him when his hand dropped away from her mouth. "I apologize, sir. You gave me quite a fright."

"Perhaps if you were not lurking in corridors where you do not belong, there would be no opportunity for such things." He frowned at her, his expression stern.

Lizzy gasped, struggling to quell her outrage. "I was not lurking anywhere, Mr. Darcy. I heard sounds of distress."

His expression didn't change. "Nonsense."

She put a hand on her hip while lifting the candelabra further aloft. Darcy's eyes squinted at the intrusion of candlelight, and she couldn't help admiring how lovely the coppery brown shade was. It was positively unfair for a man to have such gorgeous eyes and long lashes. Realizing she was distracting herself with her flights of fancy, she blinked and said, "I was not imagining it."

"No, I doubt you were. The castle is old, and I am sure you are aware we cannot patch every hole. The Bingley family has poured more money into ensuring the girls receive a quality education than bothering with small upkeep on the castle. It is likely you heard wind shrieking through a crack in the walls."

Lizzy started to argue, but as she considered it, she realized there was merit to his idea. Her cheeks flushed with heat, and she looked away. "Oh, dear. How embarrassing."

He reached out for a moment, as though he might touch her shoulder, but his hand quickly dropped to his side instead. "It is only natural to expect a period of adjustment. I have been here nearly a month, and I still find myself waking from the strange noises at night."

She tilted her head slightly. "Is that why you are about this evening, Mr. Darcy?"

He shrugged a shoulder. "I found rest unattainable, and I heard the floorboard outside my room creak. I came to investigate and saw you walking down the corridor."

She let out a shaky breath of relief. "I do apologize for disturbing you. I sincerely believed someone was in pain." As she spoke, the sound came again, clearer and louder. She frowned as she looked at him. "Are you quite certain that is the wind, Mr. Darcy?"

"I am positive, Miss Bennet, for I investigated the source myself shortly after my arrival to step in for Mr. Bingley."

After a moment, she nodded, accepting it was plausible, though she wasn't entirely convinced it was just the wind. She could see no reason why the temporary headmaster would lie to her, so she decided to accept his explanation. "In that case, I shall return to bed."

"Would you like me to walk you back to your room, Miss Bennet?"

She shook her head. "I am certain that is unnecessary. The castle is safe, is it not?"

He hesitated for a long second. "It is as long as you stay where you are supposed to." With those words, he turned faster than she would've believed possible and strode down the corridor, soon disappearing into his room.

Lizzy hesitated a moment and then started walking, following the same path but passing his room to return to the one she shared with Jane. Was it her imagination, or was his answer unnecessarily cryptic? Was he trying to scare her into staying in her room and not exploring the various nooks and crannies of Netherfield Castle? If so, Mr. Darcy did not know Lizzy, or the bounds of her curiosity.

"WAKE UP," SAID JANE with huff of impatience.

Lizzy blinked open her eyes as she realized the pale light of dawn was streaming through the window in their room. "What time is it?"

"Time to get ready, or you shall be late. Breakfast will be served in ten minutes, and Mrs. Reynolds is frightfully strict about it. She makes no exceptions for students or faculty if you miss breakfast. So hurry along, dear sister."

Smothering a yawn, Lizzy pushed back her covers and got out of bed. "I found it difficult to sleep last night after I returned to my bed."

Jane froze. "Returned? Whatever do you mean?"

Lizzy walked over to the vanity table, pouring water into her basin and using it to splash her face. It did little to help chase away the remnants of sleep. "I heard a noise that I thought was someone suffering, so went to investigate. Mr. Darcy caught me—"

"Are you in trouble, Lizzy?" Jane sounded appalled. "Mr. Darcy is ever so frightening and stern."

"I suppose he can be, but he seemed concerned and was not terribly unkind. He explained it was wind, and he had investigated it for himself upon his arrival last month." She dried her face before turning to face

Jane. "I suppose I let my imagination get the best of me." Lizzy still wasn't convinced that was the case though.

"You are braver than me. It is far safer to stay in your bed at night." Jane shivered.

Lizzy frowned. "Why is that? Is the castle dangerous?"

Jane blinked. "I do not suppose overly dangerous, but it cannot be good to be creeping around in the corridors at night. With uneven bricks in the floor and who knows what manner of dilapidation, since only the students' wing has been fully restored, it is a risk you should not take."

Lizzy accepted the wisdom of her sister's words as she pulled off her nightgown while moving around behind the dressing screen. "I do see your point, Jane, and I shall not allow my imagination to sway me next time."

"I should hope not. Your job is to teach the students, and mine is to maintain their uniforms. If there is danger skulking about, allow Mr. Darcy to handle it. He is a man, after all."

She bit back a sigh as she rolled her eyes. "Yes, and only men are capable of walking around corridors to investigate noises."

Jane apparently missed her hint of sarcasm. "I am surprised you agree, but yes."

Lizzy let it go, deciding there was no point in arguing with Jane. Her sister was being sensible as usual, but she had a point. There was no reason for the music instructor to be creeping around the halls trying to solve everyone else's ills when Mr. Darcy was apparently a light sleeper and could handle it. Yes, she would stay in her bed from now on no matter what she heard.

Chapter Two

As Lizzy moved down a hallway later that morning, she frowned at the gloom around her. Heavy drapes on the windows blocked any of the weak sunshine from filtering through, so she practically needed a candelabra to guide her way, though it was the middle of the day. Tisking her tongue with disapproval, she walked over to a panel of drapes and drew them back. After she had done so with three subsequent windows down the hall, she could actually see to walk in front of her without fear of stumbling on something.

Lizzy was opening the fifth panel of curtains when she heard a gasp behind her. She turned to look over her shoulder and barely hid a grimace. Miss Bingley, the literature professor at Netherfield Academy, stood glaring at her. She'd never been overly welcoming to Lizzy, but it was clear now she was fully displeased. "Close those at once." As she said the words, Miss Bingley rushed to the nearest panel and started to pull it shut.

Lizzy frowned at her. "But why? It is an unnecessary safety risk to have the curtains closed when it is so gloomy without them open."

"They will remain closed just in case. Do not open them again. You are new here, and it will be easy enough to sack you if you do not know how to follow rules, Miss Bennet." With those cold words, Caroline Bingley finished closing the curtains Lizzy had just opened. "Mind your place."

Lizzy didn't have a chance to verbally respond, and she knew the wise thing would be not to anyway. Miss Bingley was the sister of the former headmaster, and though Lizzy didn't know what had happened to him, she could imagine Miss Bingley still wielded a great deal of influence at the school. After all, it had been their mother who had started the endeavor, along with her close friend, or so Jane had said.

AFTER A DAY SPENT TEACHING, Lizzy met Jane in the dining hall, taking a seat at the table they were meant to chaperone. The girls spoke softly amongst themselves, and she noticed Georgiana Darcy was quiet, looking withdrawn. Concerned, Lizzy leaned over, asking, "Are you well, Miss Darcy?"

The girl blinked and then looked at her. "I am quite well, Miss Bennet. I was simply composing music in my head."

Lizzy doubted that. The girl was quite gifted on the pianoforte, as Lizzy had learned since she became an instructor at Netherfield Academy, but she could not imagine the girl looking so pensive and withdrawn just because she was mentally composing music. Still, if the pupil did not want to confide in her, she couldn't force her. Instead, she said, "If something weighs on your mind, please know you are welcome to come to me with any troubles you might have, Miss Darcy."

Georgiana's smile was more convincing this time. "Thank you, Miss Bennet. That is most kind."

After that, Lizzy returned her attention to Jane and the meal, though she felt a prickling sensation partway through. Automatically, she lifted her head and followed her instinct to identify what had caused the awareness. She looked up in time to see Mr. Darcy lingering in the doorway of the dining hall, his gaze focused on her.

Their gazes locked for a second, and her mouth went dry. Her pulse started racing, and she swore she saw his nostrils flare even from across the room, as though he detected the sudden increase in her pulse.

Convincing herself that was a mad idea, Lizzy forced herself to look away. She focused on Jane for at least another minute before allowing herself an additional glimpse, discovering Darcy had disappeared. She realized she had not seen him all day, and she was further discomforted to realize she had been looking for him, though unconsciously.

After finishing dinner, Lizzy and Jane left the dining hall, and Lizzy gasped in shock when Mr. Darcy suddenly appeared before them. She clutched her chest, and as her pulse thundered in her ears, his eyes widened, and his nostrils flared. She frowned, both at her reaction and at noticing his.

"I seem destined to frighten you at every turn, Miss Bennet," said Darcy with a tone that revealed nothing about how he regarded that.

Lizzy pressed harder against her chest, trying to slow her racing heart. "Indeed, Mr. Darcy."

"Might I have a word with you in my office, Miss Bennet?"

Lizzy glanced at Jane, almost hoping her sister would offer some excuse to rescue her. She couldn't explain why she was uneasy about being alone with Mr. Darcy, but her instincts were screaming at her to run. On the other hand, they were also screaming at her to step into his arms, so she couldn't trust her impulses now.

"I shall see you in the room, Lizzy." Jane bent her head to Mr. Darcy. "Good night, sir."

"Good night, Miss Bennet."

With Jane soon departing, she had no reason not to follow him down the corridor to the headmaster's office. She tried not to shiver with fear and something more when he gestured for her to precede him, and she heard the lock turn a moment later. The click was ominously loud in the silence.

Lizzy looked around, admiring the headmaster's office. She'd had no cause to visit yet and was surprised to discover it was surprisingly warm and cheerful. It didn't seem to fit Darcy at all, and she stared around before looking at him, trying to understand why the office was so incongruous with what she knew of Mr. Darcy.

His lips twitched, and he seemed to know where her thoughts had taken her. "Mr. Bingley decorated it, and I have had no time or reason to change his decor." He gestured toward the desk. "Have a seat, Miss Bennet."

Lizzy moved toward it, taking a seat on the velvet-upholstered hardback chair in front of the expansive mahogany desk. It reminded her somewhat of her father's desk at Longbourn, and she had to blink back unexpected tears of grief. Though it had been two years since his passing, just weeks before her departure for the musical conservatory, moments of raw grief still seized her from time to time.

When Darcy pushed in her chair gently, he put a hand on her shoulder for a flash, squeezing in a soothing fashion, as though he realized she was upset. She looked up at him uncertainly, and his hand dropped away as he moved around to sit behind the desk. "What did you wish to see me about, Headmaster Darcy?"

"You do not need to be so formal, Miss Bennet. You are not in trouble. I simply wish to remind you to abide by curfew and stay out of the dark corners of the castle. There are a great deal of repairs to undertake, and I intend to oversee many of them now that I realize how dire some are, but in the meantime, I must insist that everyone, students and teachers, stay only in the areas designated for the academy."

She swallowed, unable to resist the compulsion to say, "I was hardly somewhere forbidden last night, Mr. Darcy. I was in the staff corridor."

"I suppose, but you must stay in your room at night. Do we understand each other?" A hint of sternness was back.

Lizzy almost bowed to it and was shamed by the hint of weakness. Somehow, she managed to stiffen her spine and shoulders. "Of course, Mr. Darcy." She couldn't keep the slight note of rebellion from her tone. In an effort to distract him, she said, "You mentioned you would be undertaking the construction and repair. Why is that, Mr. Darcy?"

If he found her inquisitiveness impertinent, he was apparently willing to indulge it. "My mother and Mrs. Bingley were the ones who started this academy years ago. They believed young ladies deserved to have the sort of education offered to young men at schools like Eaton. As

I am sure you are aware, Netherfield Academy is just one of three female boarding schools open to fine families in England."

She nodded. She didn't share that she pitied some of the girls who were sent here, seeming to spend all their time, including holidays, at the school. She much preferred the method she had received for instruction as a child, where her governess taught her and her sisters at home. Still, it was a forward-thinking concept, especially since it was meant to benefit women instead of men. "You must be quite proud of that."

He nodded. "I am. Mother died before she could realize the full success of the school, but she lived long enough to see its inaugural enrolling class. Mrs. Bingley was headmistress until her retirement, and Charles stepped in then."

"I assume Mr. Bingley is your friend too, Mr. Darcy?"

He nodded. "Indeed. We have been friends for as far back as I can remember. Our mothers were quite close, so naturally, we spent a great deal of time together."

Lizzy couldn't resist the impish impulse to say, "You must be quite fond of Miss Bingley as well."

Darcy flinched for a moment, and though his expression quickly became neutral again, Lizzy saw that he did not hold Miss Bingley in high esteem by the brief betrayal of his features. "Indeed." He said the word briskly.

"That is how you came to be headmaster when Mr. Bingley disappeared?" Lizzy admitted she was indulging in more than curiosity now. She was dying to know what had happened to the previous headmaster, especially since Jane spoke of him so affectionately and with clear regard. Lizzy was uncertain if her affections had been returned, since her sister was the seamstress at the school, and that seemed a position beneath someone like Headmaster, but she had not asked Jane, for the her dear sister tended to tear up whenever the subject arose.

He scowled. "Mr. Bingley has not disappeared. I am stepping in for him for two reasons. The first is because my mother was involved with the school, and the second is because my dear sister attends."

She nodded. "I thought Miss Georgiana Darcy might be a relation of yours. I considered perhaps she was your daughter."

He frowned. "I am but ten years older than her. I could hardly be mistaken as her father."

Lizzy looked down, embarrassed. When she looked at him, he did have a youthful visage, but there was something about him that was older and worldly, suggesting he was matured far beyond his years. Perhaps that was why she'd assumed he was Miss Darcy's father instead of brother. "Of course, and my apologies, Mr. Darcy."

He let out a sound that could have been a growl. "Do not trouble yourself." He leaned back slightly. "You may go to your room now. Thank you for your time, Miss Bennet."

She got up quickly, thankful in one way to be escaping his presence, while regretful in another. She couldn't explain how he left her so conflicted, both drawn to him and frightened of him. There was something about Darcy that intrigued her even as it terrified her.

It was only as she was departing his office, having closed the door behind her, that she realized she had failed to follow up on what had happened to the previous headmaster. Darcy insisted he hadn't disappeared, but she was no closer to knowing anything more about Mr. Bingley's fate than she had before.

At least she could pass on that bit of news to Jane, if she chose, though she wasn't sure it would be worth doing so. Her sister clearly felt a great deal for the missing headmaster, and simply sharing Mr. Darcy's word that he hadn't vanished would do little to assure her sister Mr. Bingley was safe and well. Just because he hadn't disappeared didn't mean he was still alive, after all.

Chapter Three

Lizzy heard the sound again that night, and she did her best to ignore it. Really, she did. She tried putting her pillow over her ears, but she swore she could still hear the low moaning cries, and the more she listened, the more convinced she was it couldn't possibly be the wind. There was a cadence to them that suggested suffering rather than just effects of wind blowing through gaps in a stone wall.

Even after she was convinced it wasn't just wind, she did try to resist for another long minute, attempting to convince herself not to get up and explore. Mr. Darcy had warned her against it twice now, and she could ill afford to lose her position. It had been like a gift when Jane had arranged it for her all via mail when she was almost ready to leave the conservatory.

Having spent the last two years trading her tuition and board by working as a maid at the conservatory, the last thing she wanted was a career in service. She needed this instructor's position, and she would be unlikely to find such an opportunity again. No doubt, the other two boarding schools established for young ladies already had competent music teachers, and the boys' schools would certainly have employed male staff.

She would be left with the option of perhaps working as a musician or teaching private instruction if she wanted to work in music at all. If she had inconsistent bookings, she would likely end up as a lady's maid, companion, or even a governess.

All those sound reasons did little to finally sway Lizzy to stay in her bed, and she sighed with exasperation at herself when she got up, slid on her slippers, and wrapped herself in the night-rail again. As she had done the previous night, she lit the candelabra at the nightstand and took it with her, departing the room quietly.

She moved as silently as possible through the hallway this time, remembering Mr. Darcy mentioning the creaking board. As she neared his room, she eyed the floor for a second, trying to determine which one might be the culprit. There was a board that was warped compared to the rest, slightly discolored as though it had been damaged from water, and she made a wide step over it. She heard no creaking sound and continued.

The sound seemed to be coming from a different direction this time, so when she reached the bend in the corridor, she went to the left, though the previous evening, she'd thought it might be coming from the right. If it were really the wind, it was unlikely it would've changed positions.

She drew back her shoulders and took a deep breath for courage as she walked down the corridor, moving as noiselessly as possible. When she got closer, she heard definite cries of anguish, and she forgot about being quiet as she rushed forward. There was a door, partially cracked, and she pushed it open quickly so she could see what was happening.

A man thrashed on a bed with two other men doing their best to hold him down. Miss Bingley stood in the corner, and Lizzy started to ask what was happening as the other woman glared at her.

"Get out." She stormed forward, slamming the door in Lizzy's face.

Lizzy reached for the doorknob, determined to get an answer, but another hand intercepted hers, stopping her from completing the motion. She recognized the cooler touch of Mr. Darcy's hand against hers, and she shivered both from the difference in temperature and from the angry disappointment she saw in his gaze when she dared look up at him.

"I told you to stay in your room, Miss Bennet. I do not wish to have to dismiss you from your position, and your sister vouched for you. If you go, I shall have to dismiss her as well."

Lizzy gasped, opening her mouth to argue and try to save Jane's job at least, but her own natural tenacity wouldn't allow her to drop the subject. "What are they doing to that man? He sounds like he is being tortured. You must release him at once."

Darcy flinched. "It is not what you think, Miss Bennet."

She scowled up at him. "I think you are holding someone captive and hurting them. Why would you do such a thing?" She realized abruptly she was in danger as well. If they were keeping one prisoner, surely they would not hesitate to keep another—or simply dispose of her. She trembled as fear consumed her, and she took a step back.

Darcy took a step forward, maintaining the same space between them. He was looming over her now, and she swore he seemed bigger somehow. His eyes flashed, and though it must be a trick of the candlelight, there seemed to be a hint of red in his irises. "The man is being treated, not tortured."

She frowned. "What sort of treatment? I know of nothing like that."

"Perhaps, having grown up in a backwater like Meryton, there is a great deal you do not know, Miss Bennet. Return to your bed and leave this be."

"Mr. Darcy, I must insist—"

He snarled at her. It was an honest-to-goodness animalistic roar as he suddenly surged forward, pulling her into his arms. "Enough."

She stared up at him, still poised to argue, but feeling herself slip into the beauty of his eyes. They seemed to be gleaming red tonight, but that didn't detract from their utter perfection. She'd never seen something so vividly beautiful, and her mouth opened of its own accord so she could lick her lips. She could get lost in Darcy's eyes, and she was happy to do so.

He groaned again, but this was far less bestial. It was more a sound of surrender as his mouth descended, taking possession of hers.

As soon as he looked away, Lizzy was freed from his gaze, and sense started to return. It was quickly washed away again when he kissed her.

She'd never been kissed before, especially not like this. It was a soul-scorching kiss that curled her toes, and when his tongue swept into her mouth, she pressed closer. She mimicked the motions he used, her tongue stroking his before lightly dipping into his mouth.

The kiss might've continued unabated, leading perhaps somewhere very intimate, if her tongue hadn't hit a sharp point on Darcy's tooth, causing the taste of copper to fill her mouth. She gasped at the pain and pulled back, holding her mouth as she stared up at him.

"Go. To bed. Now." He seemed to be trembling, and it was quite obvious he was on the verge of losing all control.

Lizzy didn't question his words or bother to argue. She surrendered to instinct and ran, feeling like prey fleeing a predator. Even after she returned to her room, locking the door and dragging a dresser in front of it before leaning against it to pant and drag in a deep breath, she still felt hunted. There was a sense of vulnerability exposed after the kiss with Darcy.

As she slowly made her way to bed, she tried to convince herself it was simply virgin vapors, since she'd never kissed a man before. Kisses were probably often like that, and if so, she could see how women found their morals loosened long enough to indulgence in sin.

She had no doubt indulging would've been quite worth the penalty, until she remembered the sharpness of his teeth. It was almost like Mr. Darcy had fangs, and she was certain that was not normal. Perhaps she'd just been kissing him so enthusiastically that she had pressed her tongue too eagerly to his tooth, but she wasn't convinced.

Realizing the alternative was beyond belief, she shied away from contemplating it. Instead, Lizzy convinced herself she had simply been overwhelmed with passion and imagined things.

Mr. Darcy himself might've even bitten her in an attempt to dissuade her as he regained control of himself. Clearly, he was usually a man with honor, and she could not see him as the type to seduce unsuspecting teachers. Passion must have unexpectedly overwhelmed his as well, and he had no doubt been trying to help her regain control once he started to do so.

Though she didn't completely believe that narrative, Lizzy clung to it and somehow managed to fall asleep before the first blush of dawn brought light streaming into their room.

Chapter Four

Lizzy wasn't surprised to see Mr. Darcy standing in the corridor that evening when she left the dining hall with Jane. It was only a surprise that he hadn't summoned her sooner, but she hadn't seen him all day again. She frowned at that, wondering how he could be so uninvolved in the day-to-day business of the academy before reminding herself he was just a temporary headmaster. Perhaps he was uncertain how he should proceed as well.

"I would like to see you again, Miss Bennet." He sounded stiff and formal this evening, and his gaze carefully evaded hers.

Lizzy was surprised by how bereft she felt at the withdrawal of his attention as she swallowed the lump in her throat. "Of course, Mr. Darcy." She was much more reserved as she followed behind him, trying to keep an appropriate distance and then some between them.

When she was seated across from him at his desk a short time later, she folded her hands demurely on her lap and looked down, wanting to avoid his gaze. There was something almost magical about his eyes, and if she met them, looking into them too long, she would be in his thrall and lost forever. Though a fanciful flight of imagination, Lizzy couldn't help thinking there was some truth to it.

"I must apologize for my behavior yesterday evening, Miss Bennet. I had no right to kiss you."

She looked up, daring a glance at his face. Their gazes locked briefly, but there was nothing strange about his eyes this evening. They were the usual warm, beautiful brown that she so admired. Feeling a little more courage now, she swallowed again and nodded. "I kissed back, so I can hardly hold you completely to blame. I suggest we dismiss it as a moment of madness and move on."

He nodded, though she swore he seemed a little disappointed at her answer. "Of course. That is a sensible course. I am sure that if you stay out of corridors, it will not happen again."

She frowned. "Are you threatening me, Mr. Darcy?" The words had come across that way, as though he was telling her if she ventured out again, he would feel free to do as he wished with her.

He frowned. "Of course not. I was simply commenting that as long as you follow the rules, we shall have no more midnight meetings in corridors."

She sat back with a huff, wanting to argue, but also thankful he had not followed through with his threat to dismiss her, and Jane along with her. That would be a disaster for the family, since Mama, Kitty, and Lydia lived with the Gardiners in London, and Mary lived with the Philipses in Meryton. Lizzy and Jane's salaries helped their families afford to keep them.

"You are dismissed."

She started to stand but stopped in mid-motion and returned to her seat. "I would like to know more about the man, Mr. Darcy."

He sighed, sounding pushed beyond the bounds of patience, so she half-expected him to order her to leave. Instead, he ran a hand down his face, looking pale and drained for a moment. "That man is Charles Bingley. I believe you never met him?"

She shook her head. "He had already disappeared when I came to the academy, as you well know. I only know of him by what my sister has said, and she speaks highly of him."

He nodded. "Most do. Charles is...was an affable fellow, and he did not have an enemy in the world. There was an accident that has damaged his mind, and we are doing our best to help him find his way back to who he was. Right now, Mr. Bingley poses a danger to himself and others, which is why he is being held with guards. I assure you, the last thing in the world I want to do is hurt my dear friend. I am trying to help him, but he needs calm and solitude, so I must ask that you no longer investigate the noises you hear. Now that you know the source, you have no need for further information."

Lizzy couldn't help feeling disgruntled, but she nodded. It wasn't the same as a verbal agreement, and she was aware of that when she stood up. "Good evening, Mr. Darcy." Without waiting for a reply, she scurried from the room. She was a woman with a mission, needing to tell her sister what she'd learned.

She sped back to the room, unsurprised to find Jane inside. She was currently mending a pair of stockings that appeared to be fine quality, so they must belong to one of the students. She looked up from the chair where she sat, smiling at Lizzy with a hint of sympathy. "Did you survive this encounter with the headmaster, Lizzy?"

Lizzy didn't bother to answer. She rushed to Jane, kneeling beside the chair. "I have heard the most extraordinary thing from Mr. Darcy."

Jane looked up from her mending. "What?"

"Mr. Bingley is alive, Jane."

Jane let out a small cry, and Lizzy quickly realized why. She'd stabbed the needle right into her finger, and blood dripped onto the white stockings. "Oh, dear, I have ruined them. Miss Hurst will certainly insist on me replacing them, and that will probably be an entire week's wages." Jane burst into tears.

Lizzy carefully removed the white stockings, needle, and thread from her sister's hands before taking a handkerchief from her pocket to wrap the bleeding digit until blood stopped flowing. "Do not fret so, Jane. I am certain we can remove the stain. If not, we shall split the cost of replacing the stockings."

Jane nodded, and when she looked up, her eyes were filled with hope. "Is it true Mr. Bingley is really alive?"

Lizzy nodded. "I have seen him for myself, though I did not know it was him last night." She quickly told Jane what she had observed, and what she'd learned from Mr. Darcy.

Jane was scowling now. "He could have said something. We were all so worried. Charles is alive, and nobody bothered to tell me?" She seemed on the verge of tears again.

Implied familiarity at using the former headmaster's name and her reaction confirmed for Lizzy there were more to her feelings than what an employee should have for her employer. She thought no less of Jane, and she was happy to bring her the news, though it seemed to have upset her anew.

"I must see him." Jane started to stand up.

She bit her lip, torn between Mr. Darcy's words warning her to stay in her room, the impending threat of dismissal, and Jane's clear desperation. In the end, her sister won out, just as she always would. "I shall take you this evening when everyone is asleep. We have to wait until then, because if Mr. Darcy catches us, he might fire us both."

Jane sagged into the chair. "I see. I suppose I can wait a while longer."

Chapter Five

A few hours later, Lizzy and Jane crept down the hallway, this time eschewing a candelabra. They were trying to be discreet about their presence, so they were using a lone candle and the wall of the corridor to guide them, because it was very dark. None of the curtains were open, so not even moonlight could help light their way. They dared risk only the single candle, and it was proving inadequate, though it was keeping them from stumbling or getting lost.

When they reached the room he'd been in before, Lizzy hesitantly turned the knob and pushed slowly, waiting for the hinges to squeak. There was no screech, but as soon as they entered, it was obvious no one was there.

Jane looked around, clearly confused. "Where is he?"

Lizzy scowled. "They must have moved him again. I suspect they also did the first night I heard him, since the sound came from a different direction last night." She squared her shoulders. "We shall simply have to find him again, Jane. I suggest we split up to look at different doors, to hasten the prospect. Do be careful when you open them, since I believe he has guards."

"Yes, I think you are right, Lizzy." Jane was sometimes timid and normally shy, but she was clearly passionate about finding Mr. Bingley and willing to risk whatever it took. Together, the sisters left that room and split up, going different directions down the corridor.

Lizzy had managed to try three doors before she felt a presence behind her. He hadn't spoken or reached out to touch her, yet she knew Mr. Darcy was behind her even before she turned to face him, holding her candle aloft. She shivered when he blew out the wick, plunging them into darkness. "What have you done?"

"I warned you not to prowl about in corridors, Elizabeth Bennet. If you push me beyond the bounds of control, you have brought it on yourself." His voice was hoarse, but compelling.

Lizzy shivered under the intensity of it, and then shivered again when he put his cool hands on her shoulders and pulled her against him. She was expecting the feel of his lips against hers, so she was surprised when they brushed against her neck instead, his tongue reaching out to trace her carotid artery, where her pulse was frantically hammering. As his teeth grazed against it, she remembered the sharpness of his tooth that had caused her tongue to bleed, and she shuddered with a combination of fear and desire.

They both stiffened suddenly as Jane screamed—a scream of pain and fear. Lizzy jerked away, but Darcy maintained a hold on her, grasping her wrist and dragging her down the corridor with him. He moved with such grace that it appeared the utter darkness around them did nothing to slow him down. She marveled at that even as she did her best to keep up, desperate to reach her sister.

When they entered the room, there was a candelabra lit, and it revealed a gruesome sight. The blond man she'd seen the night before held Jane in his arms, but it was a parody of a lover's embrace. His mouth was buried in her throat, and blood was flowing down her sister's neck. Jane was whimpering, but it seemed to be more a sound of ecstasy than fear or pain now. Lizzy was shocked by that, and she was confused.

Darcy stormed forward, trying to pull Jane from the reluctant Mr. Bingley. He clung to her, growling and digging deeper into her throat as he tried to ward off Mr. Darcy.

"Come get her," said Darcy when he finally managed to pry off the other man's hands, his voice strained as he fought against Mr. Bingley's hold. Normally, she couldn't imagine Mr. Bingley's slighter frame would have been a match for Mr. Darcy, but there was an air of angry desperation about Mr. Bingley that seemed to lend him an advantage.

Lizzy rushed forward, grasping Jane and supporting her while she hurried her from the room. They ran down the hall, though Jane was slow and had clearly lost a lot of blood. Lizzy was still confused about what had happened, but it was clear now Mr. Darcy was correct that Mr. Bingley had lost his mind.

Lizzy led her to their room, taking one of her older petticoats and folding it into a square to press firmly against the bleeding wound on Jane's throat. "What happened?"

Jane's eyes fluttered open. "I am not entirely sure. I entered the room, and I rushed to him when I saw he was crouched on the floor. He looked so lost and alone, and I was worried for him. I put my hand out to touch his cheek, and he took my hand in his. At first, I thought it was simply because he was connecting with me, but then he brought my finger to his mouth, the one I stabbed with the needle earlier?"

Lizzy nodded, frowning at that bit of information. "Had you started bleeding again?"

"No, of course not, but I had the oddest sense he smelled the blood on me. He licked that spot a couple of times before pulling me closer. I thought he was going to kiss me, and I have missed his kisses." Jane's eyes closed.

Lizzy frowned. "You have missed his kisses?"

With a start, Jane looked up again. "I have not been entirely honest with you, Lizzy. I used to meet with Mr. Bingley in the evenings. He was never anything but a proper gentleman, aside from some kisses. Mostly, we talked and held each other. I think he was on the verge of proposing when he disappeared. I thought he was dead, but I could not show any outward signs of mourning since our relationship had not been officially recognized. To find out he was alive stirred such hope, only to discover he is...whatever he is now." She burst into tears.

Lizzy handed her a fresh handkerchief from Jane's drawer. "At least he is still alive. Perhaps the treatment he is receiving will work." It seemed doubtful if he was capable of such acts as he had committed against Jane, attacking the woman he loved, but Lizzy didn't want Jane to wallow in despair. She suspected her sister needed all her strength to recover from this wound.

"Instead of kissing me, he bit me. It hurt at first, and terribly so, but then..." She trailed off with a dreamy sigh. "It was so amazing, Lizzy. I have never felt anything like it."

"It must have been euphoria from blood loss," and Lizzy briskly. She refused to entertain any further ideas that it could be something else, though she couldn't help recalling just how mesmerized she'd felt by Darcy's gaze, and how she'd imagined flashes of red in it. No, it was utterly ridiculous to even consider such a thing.

When Jane had calmed down, and the bleeding had stopped, Lizzy left her resting peacefully. It was near dawn, but she couldn't wait to confront Darcy. She had to know what was happening, and if there was further risk to her sister.

She rushed through the corridor and pounded on the door to his room. She almost expected him to either not be there, or to ignore her. However, he opened the door moments later, positioning his body in a way that made it clear he wasn't going to invite her inside. "I need to know what is happening, Mr. Darcy."

"Later. It is too late right now. Dawn is upon me."

When he started to close the door, she put her hand out to stop it. "I must insist on an explanation. My sister is at risk, is she not?" Lizzy didn't know how she knew that, but she was sure of it. This wasn't over yet.

He frowned. "You should be fine for today. I will discuss it with you further tonight."

"Now," said Lizzy most insistently as she stomped her foot.

His lips skinned back, revealing his teeth. They were sharp and pointy, and as he growled at her, his eyes flashed red. "Tonight and not before." With those words, he slammed the door, allowing her only a second to move her arm or risk being injured.

She could've stood there and pounded on the door, trying to get him to change his mind, but she was too frightened. What he'd revealed wasn't human. Whatever plagued Mr. Bingley, she suspected it also plagued Mr. Darcy. She had to get Jane away from here.

Lizzy rushed back their room, quickly loading things into their trunks. Jane started to rouse as Lizzy was emptying her drawer. "What are you doing, Lizzy? Have we been sacked?" She sounded mournful.

"No, but we are getting out of here. There are strange goings-on at Netherfield Academy, and I believe we are in danger."

Jane's eyes closed. "I want to sleep for a while first."

Lizzy was harsh with her when she moved to the bed, forcing her sister to sit up and lightly slapping her face when Jane's eyes tried to close again. "No. You may rest in the carriage, but we are leaving. Now." Jane wasn't alert enough for Lizzy to share what she'd seen, and she wasn't certain Jane would've completely believed her if she had been fully aware, though Mr. Bingley's bite might compel her to do so. For now, she was focused on getting her sister away from the academy.

She managed to get Jane up, and she was relieved her sister had never undressed for bed, since they'd planned to seek out Mr. Bingley as soon as it was safe the night before. She wrapped her in a cloak as Jane continued to shiver, and she was worried about her sister's pallor. She put an arm around her waist and led her sister from the room. She couldn't manage Jane and the trunks, so they would have to send for their belongings.

They made it downstairs before running into anyone. When she saw Mr. Fellows, she gestured for the school's butler to approach. He eyed her with clear concern, which deepened to almost fear when he saw Jane. "Whatever is the matter, Miss Bennet?"

"My sister needs a doctor urgently. Can you please send for the school carriage?" She figured that was the easiest way to get them out of there, to imply they would be returning. Lizzy wasn't sure why, but she was half-convinced they wouldn't be allowed to leave if anyone knew why they were going.

"Of course, Miss Bennet." The butler rushed off to do her bidding, and she held Jane upright, allowing the wall to support some of her weight.

"You are not going anywhere," said Caroline Bingley from behind her.

Lizzy stiffened as she turned to face Mr. Bingley's sister. She glared at her. "I do not see how you can stop us, Miss Bingley. My sister needs a doctor."

"For one, I will refuse to allow you to take the school's carriage."

Lizzy gritted her teeth. "Very well. We shall walk from here then. We shall send for our things later." She urged Jane to stand up and lean against her. "Come on, Jane. We must leave."

"I know what happened last night, and I cannot allow you to go." Caroline sounded almost regretful for a moment when she looked at Jane. "It is not safe to take her out there."

Lizzy scoffed. "It is far less safe to leave her here at the mercy of whatever is happening in Netherfield."

"Miss Bennet, you must—"

Lizzy ignored her, urging Jane to move toward the door. Jane was mostly dead weight, and she could not imagine how they were going to cover several miles on foot, but she would worry about that once they were well away from the academy.

There was a sudden burst of pain in Lizzy's skull, and she cried out as she loosened her hold on Jane inadvertently. Her sister slumped to the floor when Lizzy stumbled forward, falling onto her hands and knees.

"I did warn you, Miss Bennet."

She looked up in time to see Caroline Bingley holding another vase over her head, clearly intent on smashing it on Lizzy's skull. That must have been what she'd done the first time as well. She lifted an arm, trying to stop her, but all it did was blunt some of the impact, and she was soon on the verge of passing out, only vaguely aware of Miss Bingley telling Mr. Fellows to lock them up before she completely lost all sense of awareness.

LIZZY WOKE LATER, REALIZING it was dark in the room she was in. It could've been artificial darkness from the heavy drapes on the windows or it could have been naturally dark. She had no way to know how long she'd been asleep.

She sat up slowly with a groan, realizing she was in a sinfully comfortable bed. With a deep breath, she recognized it smelled like Mr. Darcy, and she stiffened in fear, even as a dart of arousal went through her. She should not be responding in such a fashion to his personal scent when she knew what kind of monster he was.

"Do not be afraid, Lizzy. I am well in control this evening." Darcy spoke from a chair nearby, and she realized there was a fire lit, and three lamps were burning to provide ample illumination. They also revealed there was something in his glass, something a deep red color that made her shudder.

"What are you drinking, Mr. Darcy?"

She got slowly to her feet. She was just a little dizzy from the lingering effects of the head injury, but she was able to walk across the room and stand nearby. There was an empty chair, and it seemed to be waiting for her, but she couldn't bring herself to get that close to him yet.

"I am drinking blood. Do not be alarmed, for it has been consensually obtained. I have a number of donors who agree to be bled of a pint or two in exchange for some coins. No one is at risk of death, and there is no fear of accidental transformation this way."

"Why would you drink blood?" She sounded remarkably calm, though she was a mass of nerves on the inside.

He gave her a wry look. "It is in the nature of the beast I have become. If I do not drink blood every couple of days, it leaves me in a desperate situation, and then I become a danger."

"Like Mr. Bingley?" She hesitantly moved toward the chair, finding the courage to do so because he seemed to make no move to attack her. He appeared as calm and in control as when she'd first met him.

Slowly, she sat down, unable to hide a grimace as he brought the glass to his lips and drank. She recalled the taste of copper on her tongue when it inadvertently brushed against his fang, making her bite herself, and she wondered how he could stand it. "Do you not find it unpleasant?"

"It is distasteful in the beginning, but one grows accustomed to the flavor. At a certain point, driven by need and hunger, you start to crave it." He closed his eyes. "How I miss real food though. There was nothing like cutting into a steak, and I can never quite convince myself that blood tastes anything close to that."

She managed a ghost of a smile. "It must be frustrating. How did you come to be afflicted thusly, Mr. Darcy?"

"I must give you some history before I can explain the present, if you are agreeable?"

Lizzy nodded.

"There was a man, though of course, he started as a boy just like I did. He was the son of my father's steward, and George and I grew up almost like brothers. We were friends for a time, but as he got older, I saw the darkness inside him. When my father died, he disdained his inheritance of vicar for Kympton, which was no surprise for me. Instead, he asked for his living to be paid out in one lump sum, and I happily obliged. By that point, we had lost any closeness or friendship between us, and I simply wanted him gone.

"I wrote the check and did not think twice of it. He did not return for a few months, but when he came back, he wanted more. I gave him some money that time, but the third time he came back, eight years ago, I refused. In retaliation, he ripped out my throat and left me for dead. I do not know how it happened to him, or at what point he became a creature of the night, but Wickham was a vampire, and he turned me. I suspect he left me that way so I would be forced to change. He could have killed me by draining all my blood, but since he left blood flowing through my veins along with enough of the substance that initiates transformation, it was enough to harbor the infection, and I became what he was. A little exposure won't cause the change, but a lot makes you one of them…us."

Lizzy trembled. "It sounds horrible."

"It was. At times, it still is, though I have gained control now. I thought I had seen the last of Wickham, but he showed up a few months ago again at Pemberley, once more requesting money. Of course, I refused to give it to him, and I tried to kill him. The only way we can be destroyed is by decapitation or with a stake through the heart. I have done my research, but I did not quite aim true, and he escaped. I expected him to come after me again, but his plan was more sinister this time. Georgiana." He closed his eyes as though in pain as he said her name.

Lizzy wanted to reach out to offer comfort, but she was afraid to do so. "Did he change Miss Georgiana?"

Darcy quickly shook his head. "No, but that was his intent. He no doubt planned to kidnap her and change her, or perhaps even to marry her to force me to release her dowry. Whatever the situation, Charles interrupted it. He knows what I am, and he knows what Wickham is. I had shared my research with him, but that was because at the time I asked Mr. Bingley to end me if I became uncontrolled. I never anticipated he would be forced to go against a vampire under other circumstances."

She frowned. "What happened?" She could infer Charles had been attacked but nothing beyond that.

"With Miss Bingley's help, Charles was able to stake Wickham. He is dead, but he did not go peacefully. He bit Charles, and something has gone wrong with his transformation. Normally, a human becomes a vampire with relatively little problem, as long as they survive the physical process.

"Occasionally, the mind is damaged, and that has happened with Charles. He is like a feral animal, having lost all sense of himself and continuously gripped by the haze of bloodlust. That is why he must be kept away from everyone who is human and is under guard. Miss Jane happened to be unlucky enough to find him yesterday evening temporarily alone when the foolish guards decided to nip away for a cup of blood. That is how he was able to attack her."

Lizzy trembled as the consequences hit her. "She will become like him." She said it as a statement of fact, already knowing it wasn't a question.

He sighed and looked regretful. "Yes, Jane will become a vampire. Within hours, she will fall into a deep coma, and you will swear she is dead. At that point, you must depart the room and allow myself or one of the vampire guards to stand vigil with her. She could awaken at any point from that time, and you will be at risk as well."

Lizzy closed her eyes, a dart of grief shooting through her. "My poor sister. I have lost her."

"Not necessarily. She shall be changed and different, like me, but that does not mean she will lose her mind like poor Charles has. She could survive transformation relatively unscathed. We shall not know until she wakes again though."

"She shall wake a bloodthirsty fiend. The Jane I knew is gone."

He closed his eyes, looking weary for a moment. "There will be some adjustment, but it is not the death sentence you imagine it to be. If she regularly partakes of blood, she will remain in control of herself and not be driven to such desperation. She will be the same person she was, though her appetites and a few abilities will be altered. She will no longer be able to walk in the sunlight, and she cannot eat solid food."

"Will she be able to mesmerize people as well?" asked Lizzy, taking a guess as she recalled that thrilling moment when she'd wanted to lose herself in his eyes.

His eyes widened slightly as he nodded. "I must confess, I accidentally tried to enthrall you. I am drawn to you, Miss Bennet, which makes it more difficult to control certain aspects of my physiology. I would never wish to enslave you or take away your choice in any matter, so as soon as I realized what was happening, I tried to end it."

"Instead, you kissed me." She meant to sound accusing, but the words came out with a husky note of longing that shocked her as much as it obviously did him.

He cleared his throat, but he didn't address her tone or her words. "You should go be with Jane for now, but remember it is crucial for you to leave as soon as she enters the coma-like state and appears dead."

She got to her feet, nodding her agreement before hastily leaving his room. Her head was still throbbing, making her remember Miss Bingley's actions. She assumed the secret was why Miss Bingley had refused to allow them to leave. She'd said it was unsafe to take Jane out into the world, and now Lizzy understood why.

She was almost grateful to the other woman for having stopped her from taking Jane when she didn't understand what was happening. If Jane had turned in the forest while they were walking back to civilization, she surely would've changed or killed Lizzy as well, and she would have been an unchecked force unleashed upon anyone who crossed her path. Lizzy shuddered at the thought as she let herself into the room, intent on sitting with Jane for as long as she could.

Chapter Six

As far as Lizzy knew, Jane's transformation had happened without incident. Her sister was still reluctant to discuss it, and she was obviously still adjusting a few weeks later, but she seemed to have resigned herself to her fate. The main difference Lizzy noticed in her was they no longer ate together, and Jane slept through the days and worked at night. Lizzy didn't know where she worked, because Jane thoughtfully excused herself in the evenings when Lizzy was ready for bed, only to return shortly before dawn, when she fell into a deep sleep.

Lizzy had clearly become important to Mr. Darcy, because he continued to check in with her each day, always after dark. He had started to invite her so routinely into his office in evenings for chatting that she now went there automatically after dinner. This evening, a glass of sherry awaited her, and she knew what must be in his goblet, though it wasn't clear glass, so it obscured what he drank.

The thought was still enough to make her queasy to contemplate, but she was no longer afraid of it or him. Jane seemed to be perfectly in control as long as she regularly consumed blood, and it was clearly the same with Mr. Darcy. Only Mr. Bingley had suffered such a horrible fate from his transformation.

This evening, they moved to the chairs by the fire instead of sitting at the desk, and she took her sherry with her. "The young ladies are quite atwitter at the ball this weekend, Mr. Darcy."

He smiled. "This is the sixth such dance, from what I know. It is a tradition and Miss Bingley's idea. She believes the girls would enjoy some culture, and likely, they would not object to the young men from Eastborough Academy joining us." His eyes twinkled.

"I hear many a match has been made in the past years among our girls and boys from that academy at the annual ball." She sipped the sherry, which was superb quality. It always was.

"Yes, I have heard the same. I have never experienced one, but it appears to be one way a great many students meet boys who interest them and become husbands in the future."

"I must confess, I am excited as well. The most glamorous ball I ever attended was at the Assembly in Meryton, but I miss those. I am certain you would find it far too rusticated, and with no woman handsome enough to please you, but it was quite a diversion for our area."

"If you were there, I am certain I would have found the handsomest woman in the room to dance with." His eyes were saying more than his mouth, and they were seductive. They were enough to draw her in, but it didn't feel like that artificial mesmerism she had experienced before. This was a truly organic experience, and she was finding it difficult to look away.

He cleared his throat, his eyelids shuttering his gaze for a moment. "Since you will be there, I would like to request two dances reserved on your card, Miss Bennet."

She smiled. "I can imagine what gossip that might ignite among the young ladies."

He looked pained. "Believe me, I shall be dancing with all the ladies on staff, including Miss Bingley." He seemed to dread the idea.

Lizzy could not help her curiosity. "It seems strange to me that you and Miss Bingley are not closer, since your families are so interwoven, and you have grown up together."

"That is precisely why we are not. I have seen the best and worst of Miss Bingley, and she is more like a bratty little sister to me than anyone I could regard as a marriageable match. It is the same for me with my sweet cousin, Anne. My aunt, Lady Catherine de Bourgh, wants me to marry her, but even if I were not hiding the affliction I have, I could never bring myself to wed her. I have brotherly affection for her and nothing more."

Lizzy nodded. "I quite understand. There was a brief visit from a cousin of ours, the one who inherited Longbourn in the entailment. Jane was lucky enough to be in London and never met him, so his attentions fell on me. When I refused his offer of marriage, he married my friend Charlotte instead, but he was quite spiteful. Papa had not been dead a fortnight before he showed up with all his belongings and told us we had to leave Longbourn."

He frowned. "Mr. Collins and his wife, Charlotte? I do believe I know them. He served as vicar for Rosings Park, my aunt's estate, for a time."

She nodded. "It does sound like him, and the name Rosings Park is familiar."

"A most disagreeable fellow. I am glad you were able to escape that fate."

Lizzy sipped her sherry again. "As am I, though Mama took to her sick bed for a full week to bemoan how shortsighted and ungrateful I was." She looked up. "Were you aware Jane is spending a lot of her evenings with Charles? She just told me yesterday."

He nodded. "I heartily approve. She is in no danger now that she is like him. Vampires do not feed on each other...at least not for sustenance." There was a strange tone in his voice, and his eyes darkened for a moment.

Lizzy shivered, aware of a new atmosphere in the room. It seemed to be laden with sensuality, and for some reason, she could envision Mr. Darcy biting her wrist before soothing the spot with a kiss. She trembled, not certain if it was from fear or longing, or a strange mix of both.

She cleared her throat. "She tells me Mr. Bingley is making some progress. He is no longer quite so wild and seems to answer to his name now. They were in love before his attack." She shared the information with an air of expectation, wanting to see how he would react, since there was a marked difference in Jane's social status versus Mr. Bingley's.

"I believe she was the mysterious woman he referenced in his letters a few times, the one whose beauty was beyond compare, and who is the soul of kindness herself." He smiled. "I am happy for them if he can recover enough to have the future they planned."

Lizzy sipped her sherry again. "Of course, my sister and I come from far humbler roots than Mr. Bingley." And the Darcys, though she left that unspoken.

He shrugged a shoulder. "I do not see that it matters, especially trapped in a life such as ours."

She couldn't help but laugh then. "Perhaps you would change your mind if you met my mother."

His lips twitched. "Perhaps, but I cannot see that she would be such a deterrent as to make me want to dissuade Charles from happiness. Or myself."

THE NIGHT OF THE BALL, Lizzy wore the dress Jane had helped her sew, since her sister had always had a better hand and eye for that sort of thing. Jane was attending as well, though she had been reluctantly recruited to do so. She hated to leave Mr. Bingley alone even for an hour or two, but Lizzy had insisted, knowing Jane needed to get out of that stuffy room for a while and interact with others.

Besides, she'd been seen so infrequently by the students that they were starting to gossip and speculate she had disappeared as well. Jane needed to make an appearance to show the girls there was no nefarious force moving around the castle kidnapping various people. That was the latest theory she'd heard from Miss Darcy, and it was clear Georgiana had no idea what her brother was. Lizzy imagined that would change when she got older, but she understood and maintained his discretion for the time being.

They entered the ballroom, and she saw several young men from the Eastborough Academy. They had arrived in a string of coaches all afternoon and would be staying over at the castle, but in a separate wing with a great many chaperones to prevent any impropriety. For now, everyone was dancing in a dignified fashion, though the sound of giggles certainly rose above the musicians' instruments.

She let out a startled gasp when a chilly hand brushed against her back, though she recognized Darcy's presence before she even turned her head. She'd become attuned to him, and she no longer found that strange. She smiled at him in welcome. "It is good to see you this evening, Mr. Darcy."

"You as well, Miss Elizabeth." He turned to Jane, taking her hand in a concerned fashion. "How are you this evening, Miss Jane? Are you well?"

Jane nodded. "I am quite well. I will not stay long though. I have matters to which I must attend." Her look spoke volumes.

Darcy nodded. "Indeed."

Caroline Bingley approached them then, and she was a vision in a lovely ivory gown that Lizzy knew Jane had sewn for her. Caroline had paid her well for it, so she could hardly begrudge the woman taking advantage of Jane's talents since Lizzy had done the same.

It was a startling contrast to her lovely auburn hair, which was arranged in a series of curls to drape over her left shoulder. Caroline Bingley was a classic beauty, but there was a haughty expression on her face that never seemed to change. She glanced at Lizzy almost dismissively. "What an unusual dress."

She scowled, knowing there was nothing wrong with her dress. "Yes, Jane designed it, just as she did yours."

Mr. Darcy sounded like he might laugh, but he quickly changed it to a cough as Caroline grimaced. She turned to Mr. Darcy. "I have several dances remaining on my card, Mr. Darcy. Would you like to reserve two?"

"I shall certainly reserve one, Miss Bingley. I have a great many people to dance with this evening. Obligations, you know."

Caroline nodded, looking as though she'd sucked on a piece of lemon at the news he didn't want two of her dances. "Of course. Duty and obligation force you to dance with others." She gave Lizzy a scathing glance.

"Yes, though I am anticipating some of the evening ahead." He turned to Lizzy, taking her hand. "Shall we, Miss Bennet?"

Lizzy really tried not to shoot a smug look at Caroline Bingley as she took Darcy's hand and walked with him onto the dance floor when the musicians started another song. She was trying to be a good person, but even she was unable to completely resist the urge to glance a little arrogantly at Caroline Bingley when that song ended, and Mr. Darcy continued dancing with her for the next one.

Mr. Darcy took advantage of a moment when they were facing each other to whisper, "Will you come to my room tonight, Lizzy? There is something I wish to discuss with you."

Perhaps she should have felt a shiver of fear, but she didn't. Mr. Darcy seemed well-controlled, and if he were intent on ravishing her, she couldn't pretend she would put up much of a fight. No fight at all, to be honest. She wanted Mr. Darcy, and she didn't care about the propriety of it.

She had no plans to marry, so what would it matter if she slept with him? Surely, being a man of the world, he would know ways to prevent pregnancy, which was her sole concern. Perhaps vampires could not even reproduce anyway.

She nodded her agreement and moved away from him, spending the rest of the ball in tense anticipation. She watched him dance with others, including Caroline Bingley, who seemed entirely too forward. Her jealousy was unwarranted, but she couldn't help feeling it anyway. The more she watched Mr. Darcy, the more she could not escape a startling realization. She was in love with him. Perhaps it should matter that he was a creature of the night, but her heart didn't care, so she allowed herself to release any concerns or fears for loving such a man.

43

Chapter Seven

Lizzy met him in his room, feeling a hint of nervousness, but mostly anticipation. He closed the door behind her, taking her hand to draw her over to the fire.

He didn't sit down this time though. Instead, he took her hands in both of his and stared down at her earnestly. "I have tried to fight how I feel, Lizzy. It is unfair of me to want a future with any woman, but you know what I am, and I hope you can overlook my deficiencies. I promise I will not be a burden to you, and you will make me the happiest man in the world if you will accept my proposal. Will you marry me?"

Lizzy gasped, eyes widening. "You called me here to propose?" She frowned up at him. "I did not expect this."

He looked crestfallen, and his hands loosened around hers. "I am sorry to spring such an unpleasant thing upon you. I shall endeavor to eliminate any tender feelings for you and leave you be, Miss Bennet." He turned away from her.

Lizzy sighed impatiently as she put a hand on his shoulder, urging him to look at her. "I did not refuse. I was simply surprised. I thought you had invited me here for seduction. I did not realize you planned to make an honest woman of me first, Mr. Darcy."

His eyes widened. "You believed I would be so dishonorable?"

Her lips twitched. "I rather hoped you would be. If I accept your proposal, and I have every intention of doing so, surely you will not make me wait until we are married to have our wedding night?" As she spoke, she trailed her fingers down his chest before moving to the ties on the front of her gown. She untied them slowly before turning around. "Will you unbutton me, Mr. Darcy?"

There was a moment of hesitation, as though he was warring with himself. When he groaned and his fingers brushed against her skin as he started undoing the buttons, Lizzy knew he had lost the battle as he finished unfastening the buttons before sitting down. His eyes darkened with passion, and he reached for her, pulling her onto his lap.

She melted into his embrace, eager to belong to him completely. Soon, she would be his wife in every sense of the word. She experienced no hesitation when his mouth slanted over hers. Lizzy parted her lips to allow his tongue inside her mouth, shyly touching it with her own. Her body tingled with warmth, and a pit of lava burned in her stomach, sending heat spiraling through her body. Her thighs quivered when Fitzwilliam rested his hands on them.

He stroked the soft material of her gown, gradually pulling it up her legs until her stocking-clad calves were revealed. Lizzy undid the buttons of his waistcoat, running her fingers along the smooth satin. When it hung open, she went to work on the shirt, until it was opened to his waist, where the hem disappeared into his breeches. She was nervous but excited to see his body bared to her.

Fitzwilliam's hands trembled slightly when he pulled the dress from her shoulders and let it fall to her waist. His hands were warm through the thin cotton of her shift, and she arched her back, offering him more. He dipped his head to suckle one of her nipples through the cotton, abrading the tender peak in a manner that had her close to screaming at the gratifying sensation.

When he lifted his head, he rubbed the wet material against her nipple, further agitating the bud, making Lizzy bite her lip. She wanted to cry out her pleasure, but she feared the staff nearby might hear her. "Stop teasing me."

He grinned at her, letting his hand move down the front of her shift with sensuous slowness. "Very well, dear Lizzy." He made quick work of stripping off the shift once she lifted her hips before tossing it over his shoulder. She remained in just her chemise and petticoat. "What shall I do next?"

She frowned at him. It wasn't like Fitzwilliam to be so playful, especially since he must have realized how she was yearning to completely join with him. "Make me yours."

His grin faded, and he pulled her more snugly onto his lap. "You already are, Lizzy." With tender urgency, Fitzwilliam stripped off her chemise. "Lean forward."

Bracing her hands on his shoulders, Lizzy lifted her bottom into the air to allow him to take off the petticoat. When she sat on his lap again, her bare buttocks rested on the fall of his breeches. A laugh escaped her when she looked down to see she still wore her slippers and nothing else. With a flip of each ankle, she kicked them off before clamping her thighs around his waist. "You wear too many clothes, Fitzwilliam."

He grunted. "I agree, but I have no wish to part from you to remove them."

"Allow my assistance." Lizzy pushed off his waistcoat before tugging his shirt from his opened breeches to undo the last button and slide it off as well. She nibbled on her tongue, considering the logistics of removing his breeches with him seated and her sitting atop him.

Fitzwilliam took over, sliding her from his lap so he could remove his boots and strip off the breeches and drawers. When he was nude, he beckoned her close again, and she settled back onto his lap.

She gasped when Fitzwilliam leaned forward, laying her on the floor before the fireplace in one smooth movement. Lizzy clutched his shoulders as he shifted to kneel between her thighs, and his face nestled against her stomach. She loosened her grasp and moved one hand to his head, to stroke his curls. "What are you doing?" she asked when he kissed her stomach.

"Tasting you." Her stomach quivered under the teasing touch of his lips as he kissed her again, gradually moving lower. Instinctively, she stiffened. "Be calm, love. I will never hurt you." With that, he bent his head, and seconds later, she flinched when his fangs penetrated her skin.

She rose up to see Fitzwilliam, eyes wide when she saw he was feeding from the vein in her thigh. The pain had faded quickly, replaced by incredible bliss that flooded through her in warm waves, and she comprehended how Jane had ended up enjoying having Mr. Bingley feast on her blood.

She laid down again, losing herself in the soft sounds of his sucking, the faint copper odor of blood mingled with the scent of her arousal, and the beating of her heart lulling her into a semi-trance as it slowed. Slowly, his fangs retracted, and his focus shifted from her thigh to her core.

Lizzy stiffened, afraid he would bite her in that tender spot, but he just traced his tongue up and down her slit before circling her pearl. She surrendered to the ecstasy he brought her, soon feeling a release crash over her. She had to bite hard on her tongue to keep from crying out in her release.

When he lifted his head a few minutes later, a trickle of her blood marred his chin, but there was little else to prove he had been supping from her. Lizzy held out her arms, too content to speak, and he came to her.

He kissed her lips, merely brushing his against hers, but Lizzy lifted a hand to hold him against her while she deepened the kiss. The lingering taste of her blood and fluid was unpleasant, but she kept kissing him, sweeping her tongue around his mouth, determined to show she accepted him for what he was. When she finally chose to break the kiss, she said, "Make love to me now."

"I shall endeavor to make it pleasurable for you." His hand slipped between their bodies to prepare her for his entrance. "I do not want to hurt you..."

Lizzy touched a finger to his lips. "Do not fret." She braced herself for pain when the head of his shaft pressed against her opening before he surged inside her. It was uncomfortable, but not intolerable. Soon, his thrusts incited more pleasure than pain, and her hips rose to meet each one. Their rhythm was easy to find, as if they had established it long ago.

Her body geared up for release, shaking with the strength of her impending orgasm. Lizzy bit hard on her tongue to restrain a cry, somehow managing to breathe as her world fell apart and reformed in the space of a few flashes. Amazingly, this release was even more intense than the one he'd given her with his mouth.

Afterward, they laid together in contentment for a long time, with Fitzwilliam careful not to brace his full weight upon her. Lizzy rested her head on his shoulder, breathing in his scent, and contemplating how complete she was. How had she lived twenty-three years without him? She didn't care what he was. She only knew she couldn't return to an existence that didn't feature Fitzwilliam.

Chapter Eight

Lizzy was leaving Fitzwilliam's room later that night, the ruby ring from the Darcy vault snug on her left finger as she crept down the hallway toward the room she still shared with Jane. They would have to maintain the pretense of that until she and Fitzwilliam were married, but they had no intention of waiting long.

She smiled, recalling they couldn't afford to anyway, since they had not bothered to use any form of protection, and she had learned from him that vampires were not only not sterile, but were often quite virile. Even now, she could be carrying his child, and the idea filled her with pleasure.

She stiffened as she heard a creak behind her, realizing it was the board in front of Darcy's room. She turned her head, half-expecting Fitzwilliam to be standing there, reluctant to let her go though it was nearly dawn, but instead, it was Caroline Bingley. The woman looked distraught, with tear tracks on her face, and her carefully coiffed hair was a mess. She still wore the gown from earlier, but even it was in a state of dishabille.

Lizzy moved toward her. "Miss Bingley, are you unwell?"

"He is mine. He was always supposed to be mine. His mama and my mama often mentioned their fond desire to have us join the Bingley and Darcy families officially. He is meant to marry me. What you had with him tonight means nothing. He is still going to marry me." Her eyes glittered with rage.

Lizzy scowled at the other woman. "No, he is not." She lifted her hand to show Caroline the ring. "Fitzwilliam and I are engaged. I shall not mention this to him to keep you from humiliation, but you simply must cease to believe there is something more between the two of you. He regards you as a sister and nothing more."

"Lies." Caroline was clearly enraged, and she bore down on Lizzy.

Lizzy was one for standing her ground, but there was something terribly intimidating about Caroline in this state. She reminded Lizzy of Charles at his worst, and she feared she saw a streak of madness in the other woman. Before she could decide how to proceed, Caroline was bearing down on her.

Lizzy opened her mouth to scream as she turned to run, not making it very far before Caroline shoved against her. Lizzy was too close to the stairs, and she teetered for a moment, hoping she could maintain her balance as Fitzwilliam's door opened, and he rushed out. She knew he was fast, and she prayed he would reach her in time, but as he rushed toward her, Caroline pressed hard against her back, and Lizzy lost her balance, plunging down the stone stairs.

Incredible pain filled her during the descent, but as she landed, she could feel nothing at all. She was numb, and if she was moving her limbs, she couldn't feel it. The only pain was in her neck, and it was unbearable, along with agony in her skull from where she had collided with the stone steps several times. Blood obscured her vision, but she still recognized Darcy as he leaned over her, gathering her into his arms.

"My love. You shall be all right."

She wanted to lift her hand to touch him, to soothe and reassure him, but she couldn't get it to move. "I shall not be. I do love you, Fitzwilliam. Never doubt that."

He seemed frantic, and when he looked at Caroline, his teeth bared in a feral growl. "I will kill you."

"No, Fitzwilliam. She is ill. There is something wrong with her mind. You must send her away where she can get care, but do not retaliate for this. She acted in rage, not dispassionate calculation."

He appeared on the verge of tears. "Even now, you can think of her instead of yourself?"

She smiled. "I am not that selfless, my love. I simply do not wish you to carry the burden of having done away with Caroline Bingley on your conscience for eternity." Her eyes closed, and she could feel what little strength she had ebbing from her body.

"Lizzy, I am going to bite you. It could be that you are too far gone, but maybe the bite will save you, and if it does, the change will heal you. Is that what you want?"

Lizzy's eyes fluttered open, and she blinked a couple of times, but she couldn't manage the strength to say yes or no. She was relying on Darcy to choose for her, but she couldn't even convey that as her eyes closed again.

Epilogue

The tumescent moon was brighter and more beautiful than Lizzy had ever seen, but she had a new appreciation for sights and sounds now that she was a vampire. It heightened her senses in ways she hadn't expected, and she processed everything around her with a new zest, especially since she had come perilously close to losing it all.

She'd been changed for three weeks now, and she was adapting to the process. It was a good thing she was about to marry Fitzwilliam, because it explained why she would no longer be teaching the girls. She could find no way to structure her schedule that would allow after-dark classes, and a vampire was compelled to sleep during the day. Instead, she would do what she could to help with running the school for the next few weeks before she and Fitzwilliam departed for Pemberley.

Charles stood nearby, his arm around Jane. He was clearly recovered, and though he'd had a difficult time adjusting to his new reality in the beginning when his mind returned, especially the knowledge he had been the one to change Jane without her consent, he was adapting well now.

Fitzwilliam thought, and Lizzy concurred, that by the time he and Jane spent a month in Italy for their honeymoon, Charles would return invigorated and ready to run the school again. That would allow them to take their own honeymoon before returning to Pemberley.

First, they had to be married. She put her arm through Darcy's as Mr. Fellows led the vicar to meet them in the school's garden with Miss Georgiana trailing behind. She appeared excited to be included in the secret midnight ceremony, and she had taken news of her brother and his friends being vampires with surprising calm.

The vicar looked antsy, but Fitzwilliam had paid him handsomely to come. He still stared at them with surprise and a little bit of suspicion as he joined them in the gazebo. "This is most peculiar, Mr. Darcy. Most peculiar. Marriages are always done on Saturday and Wednesday mornings."

"It is at your discretion to do otherwise, sir, and you have accepted compensation for your inconvenience. This was the only time that would work for us." Fitzwilliam allowed no further argument.

With a spluttering sound, the vicar opened his Bible and placed it on the dais that was prepared for him. There were lit torches providing ample light, though he likely had the passages memorized anyway.

Lizzy turned to face Darcy as the ceremony began, aware of Jane's back near hers. She stood facing her soon-to-be husband as well, one hand on Charles's chest. Lizzy listened to the vicar drone on, wishing he would speed up the process a little. She was looking forward to the wedding night far more than the wedding.

Fitzwilliam had denied her further pleasures until they were married, claiming he didn't want them to be discovered and set a bad example for the girls at the school. She understood that, but she was crazy with frustration, and she could hardly wait for the night ahead of them.

"I pronounce you husband and wife and husband and wife. You may kiss the brides."

She lifted her head to kiss Fitzwilliam as Mr. Fellows and Georgiana stepped forward to sign the certificate as witnesses. Lizzy knew he had explained the situation to Georgiana a few days ago, and she was already asking Darcy to change her, but he had refused to do so until she had a few more years of experience in life and was certain that was what she wanted.

She admired his restraint in sticking to his principles. As it were, she was already planning to change her mother and sisters if they requested it, once she found a way to tell them. She only wished she'd had the opportunity to offer her father such a gift before his passing.

She blinked away the moment of melancholy as Darcy kissed her again before pulling her into his arms and sweeping her off her feet. It was quite a walk from the garden to their room, but she knew he had the stamina for it, so she simply clung to him as he whisked her away to their bedchamber and made her his wife in every sense of the word.

PLEASE SIGN UP FOR Abbey's newsletter[1] to receive information about new releases. If you have any difficulties, email Abbey to request a manual add.

---

1. https://www.subscribepage.com/JAFF

Author's Note

I took a few liberties with the original idea and personalities to make this work, but I hope it retains enough of ODC to be enjoyable.

About The Author

Abbey is a diehard Jane Austen fan and has loved Fitzwilliam since the first time she "met" him at age thirteen upon borrowing the book from the school library. He is the ideal man, though Abbey's husband is a close second. Abbey enjoys writing various steamy and sweet Jane Austen variations, but "Pride & Prejudice" (and Mr. Darcy) will always be her favorite.

Did you love *Shadow of Darcy: A Sensual Pride & Prejudice Paranormal Variation*? Then you should read *Darcys' First Christmastide*[1] by Abbey North!

[2]

Christmastide with a touch of magic...

When Lizzy and Fitzwilliam argue about Lady Catherine on their first Christmastide together, Lizzy impulsively flees to the grounds. Walking is her solace, but she soon walks into an unexpected snowstorm. Fitzwilliam searches for her, but it takes an unexpected source of help to reunite the married couple and ensure their holiday is merry and bright.

---

1. https://books2read.com/u/3kYqAK

2. https://books2read.com/u/3kYqAK

Also by Abbey North

A Month To Love
Reproach (Part One)
Resentment (Part Two)
Rapport (Part Three)
A Month To Love Compilation

Crime & Courtship
Rapacity & Rancor: A Pride & Prejudice Variation
Abduction & Acrimony : A Pride & Prejudice Variation Mystery Romance
Extortion & Enmity: A Pride & Prejudice Variation Mystery Romance
Murder & Misjudgment: A Pride & Prejudice Variation Mystery Romance
Perfidy & Promises: A Pride & Prejudice Variation Mystery Romance
Crime & Courtship: A Sweet Pride & Prejudice Mystery Romance Compilation

Darcy's Courtesan
Adversity (Darcy's Courtesan, Part One)
Avidity (Darcy's Courtesan, Part Two)

Amity (Darcy's Courtesan, Part Three)
Darcy's Courtesan: A Sensual "Pride & Prejudice" Variation

Marriage & Mysteries
Honeymoon & Hemlock

Mr. Darcy's Secret Stories
Mistaken Masquerade: A Pride & Prejudice Variation
Mischief & Matchmaking: A "Pride & Prejudice" Variation

Standalone
Christmas At Pemberley: A Pride & Prejudice Variation
A Scandalous Proposition: A Pride & Prejudice Variation
Shadow of Darcy: A Sensual Pride & Prejudice Paranormal Variation
Darcy's Obsession
Blackmailing Lizzy: A "Pride & Prejudice" Variation
Darcy's Wicked Game
Danger With Darcy: A Sensual "Pride & Prejudice" Variation
Passion & Prostrations: A Sensual "Pride & Prejudice" Variation
Darcy's Debt: A Sensual Pride & Prejudice Variation
Obstinacy & Obligation: A Sweet Pride & Prejudice Variation
Follies & Foibles: A Sweet "Pride & Prejudice" Variation
Heartsick: A Sweet "Pride & Prejudice" Variation
Darcy's Alibi: A Sweet "Pride & Prejudice" Variation
Darcy's Runaway Bride: A Sweet "Pride & Prejudice" Variation
Never A Bride: A Fade-To-Black "Pride & Prejudice" Variation
Marooned With Darcy: A Sensual "Pride & Prejudice" Variation
Compromising Mr. Darcy: A Steamy "Pride & Prejudice" Variation

Marrying Mr. Darcy: A Sensual "Pride & Prejudice" Variation
To Dance With Darcy: A Sweet "Pride & Prejudice" Variation
Darcys' First Christmastide

9 798215 018804